For Mark, thanks for your
belief and support ~ T.C.

For Laura and my family, thanks for
all the support! Love you guys ~ T.N.

tiger tales
5 River Road, Suite 128, Wilton, CT 06897
Published in the United States 2018
Originally published in Great Britain 2018
by Little Tiger Press
Text copyright © 2018 Tracey Corderoy
Illustrations copyright © 2018 Tony Neal
ISBN-13: 978-1-68010-102-7
ISBN-10: 1-68010-102-1
Printed in China
LTP/1400/2181/0318

For more insight and activities, visit us at www.tigertalesbooks.com

The Christmas EXTRAVAGANZA Hotel

by
TRACEY CORDEROY

Illustrated by
TONY NEAL

Far from the hustle and bustle of town,
Bear was ready for a nice, simple Christmas.
His cozy fire popped and danced,
and his candle cast a golden glow.
But as he opened his favorite book,
he heard a loud

Beep! Beep!

Bear looked up.
"Who could that be?"

"Hello!" said a cheery little frog.
"I've arrived for my Christmas

EXTRAVAGANZA!
Show me the lights! The tree!
The flying reindeer! Let's get
Christmas started!"

Frog waved a brochure under Bear's nose.
"The Christmas Extravaganza Hotel?" read Bear.
"I think you have the wrong place."
"No! No!" Frog tapped the map.
"It's right here, see?"
Bear looked closer. "Oh! Your map's
upside-down. That hotel is on the
other side of the world."

"But . . . it CAN'T be!"
wailed Frog. "I had it all
planned — I've even knitted a
hat, look! Now I'll never get
to my hotel in time for
Christmas!"

Bear thought very hard.
"You could always stay with . . .
umm . . . me?" he said kindly.
"I'm going to have a
wonderful Christmas!"

"You ARE?"
Frog brushed his tears away.
"Hooray!"

So he hopped on in, drank a HUGE mug of hot chocolate, then dozed off by Bear's cozy fire.

As Frog slept, Bear flipped through the brochure. "A singing tree?" he gasped. "A supersonic sleigh ride? Frog won't find that here!"

"Bear! Bear!" called Frog the next morning.
"Can we please start our Christmas
EXTRAVAGANZA?"
"Of course," yawned Bear.
So Frog checked the brochure . . . . "Ooo, so do you have
an all-you-can-eat North Pole breakfast bar?"
"Not exactly," replied Bear. "But we could make iced cookies!"
"Really?? With Christmas sprinkles?
Show me! Show me!!"
Frog cried.

Bear handed him an apron,
and they started to bake.

And although it wasn't
exactly like the brochure,
Frog liked it!

But suddenly, Frog looked around.
"Bear, where is your Christmas
tree?" he asked. "My brochure
has a BIG one — that sings!"
Smiling, Bear led Frog
outside . . . .

"How about this one?" he asked.
Frog looked up . . . .
and up . . . and UP! "WOW!"
Bear's beautiful tree twinkled with frost.
"And look!" cried Frog as two little robins
hopped about, chirping brightly.
"It even has singing decorations!
And . . . . SNOW! Do you have a
snow machine?"
"No! No!" chuckled Bear.
"That's real snow!"

Frog soon found he loved
real snow. And long walks
through the woods.

And picnic lunches!

Frog found footprints
in the snow.
"Let's follow them,"
smiled Bear.

And they found three **real** reindeer!
"Now we can have a sleigh ride!!" exclaimed Frog.
But Bear shook his head.
"I'm sorry, but these aren't Santa's reindeer,"
he said. "And I don't have a sleigh."

But Bear knew **exactly** what Frog would like instead . . . .

"Snowball fight! Hooray!!" cheered Frog. "And that's not even in the brochure!"

They played until the sky turned inky blue.
"And now for the BEST part!" Frog cried. "It's time to turn on the Christmas lights!"

He pulled out his brochure
and showed Bear a photo
with strings and strings of
lights, flashing away.

Christmas
EXTRAVAGANZA

HOTEL

"Oh," Bear sighed.
His Christmas lights
weren't like those.

Bear hurried home and lit all of his candles.
"Will these lights work?" he asked.
Frog blinked. They weren't quite the
EXTRAVAGANZA
he'd expected. But Bear had been so kind . . . .

"Why . . . yes!" exclaimed Frog, putting on a big smile.
"So . . . ummmm . . . Christmassy!"

They watched the golden flames in silence.
Then suddenly Bear's eyes lit up.
"Follow me, Frog!" he said, grabbing hats and scarves . . . .

"What about these lights?" Bear pointed to the sky.
"Oh, Bear!" gasped Frog, "They're perfect!"

When they went back inside, Frog said, "What a magical day!" And it wasn't over yet . . . .

"Shhh!" whispered Bear. "What's that jingling? It's coming from the rooftop."

Frog checked the brochure — not a THING about jingles!

"It must be Santa!" Bear exclaimed. "But we need to go to sleep — quickly!"

They dove under the blankets and shut their eyes tight.

"Psst, Bear! Are you sleeping? I am!" chattered Frog.

But Bear was already snoring . . . .

On Christmas morning, there was a huge present by the fire. "Bear!" squealed Frog. "Look! It's from Santa! He came!"

From Santa

They each took an end of the ribbon and pulled. "A sleigh!" beamed Bear. "Why, Frog — this is just what we need . . .

. . . for our sleigh ride!"
"SUPERSONIC!" cheered Frog.
"Can I come back again next year?
Your Christmas Hotel is the BEST!"

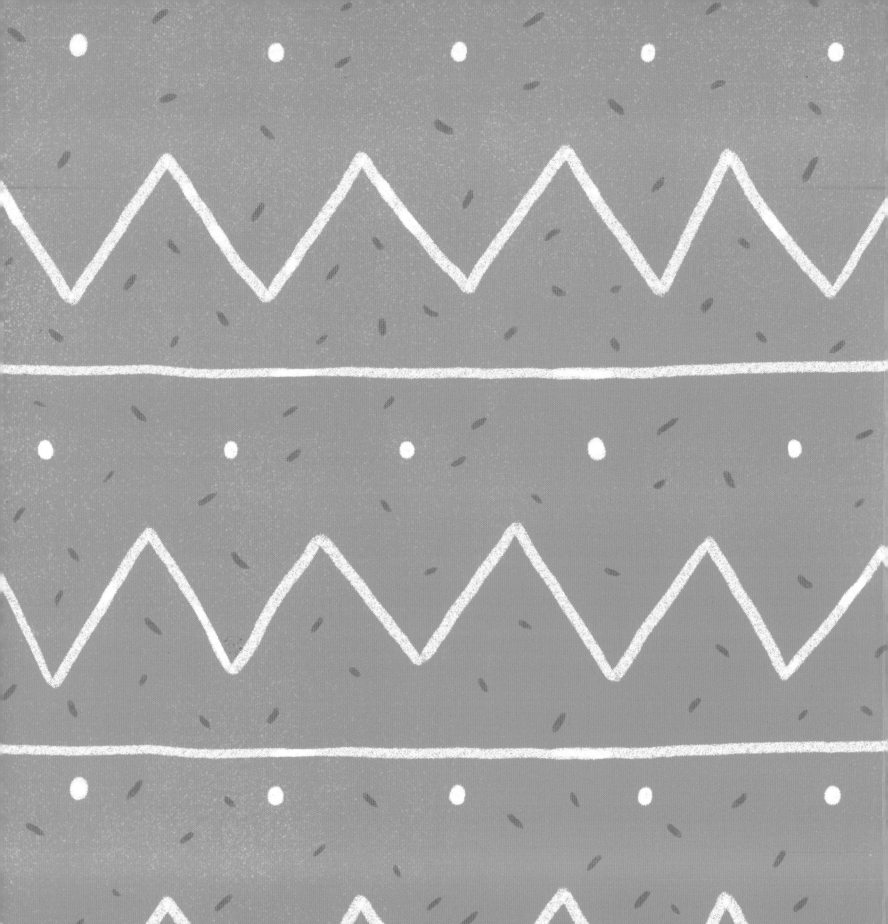